Dancing Dreams

and other stories

By Helen Bailey and Emma Thomson

Illustrated by Emma Thomson

How to make your felicity Wishes.

WISH

With this book comes an extra special wish for you and your best friend.

Hold the book together at each end and both close your eyes.

Wriggle your noses and think of a number under ten.

Open your eyes, whisper the numbers you thought of to each other.

Add these numbers together. This is your

Magic Number

you

best friend

Place your little finger on the stars, and say your magic number out loud together. Now make your wish quietly to yourselves. And maybe, one day, your wish might just come true.   Love

felicity

x

For Buttercup, Whitstable, Kent.

E.V.T

For Gillian Charles — Always a beacon
of support and encouragement.

H.E.B

FELICITY WISHES © 2002 Emma Thomson
Licensed by White Lion Publishing.

Dancing Dreams and Other Stories text © 2002 Helen Bailey and Emma Thomson
Illustrations copyright © 2002 Emma Thomson

First published in Great Britain in 2002 for WHSmith,
Greenbridge Road, Swindon, SN3 3LD
by Hodder Children's Books

The rights of Emma Thomson and Helen Bailey to be identified as the authors
and Emma Thomson as the illustrator of this work have been asserted by them
in accordance with the Copyright, Designs and Patents Act 1988.

10 9 8 7 6 5 4 3

A Catalogue record for this book is available from the British Library

ISBN 0 340 85586 X

Printed and bound in Great Britain by Bookmarque Ltd, Croydon, Surrey.

CONTENTS

* * ✳ * *

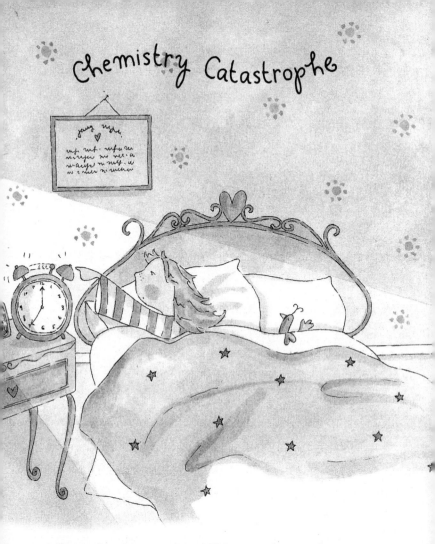

Chemistry Catastrophe

The alarm went off at 7am. Felicity Wishes woke up, rolled over, and opened one eye just enough to see the clock to turn it off, before snuggling back under her warm, pink duvet.

Every night she went to bed with the intention of getting up early and getting to school on time and every morning when her alarm went off she changed her mind.

"Why is it," she thought sleepily, "that beds seem so unappealing when it's time to go to bed and so appealing when it's time to get up? Life would be so much easier if it were the other way around!"

Felicity reached out from under the covers to pick up the school timetable from her bedside table. Double Science followed by Practical Wish-Making. She loved going to the School of Nine Wishes and seeing her friends but somehow, despite her best intentions, her lessons never went according to plan. In her last end of term report, Fairy Godmother had written: "Felicity Wishes is a delightful fairy, popular with her classmates, polite and helpful. However, she *must* try to concentrate more in class."

Felicity pulled the covers over her head as she thought back to the start of school. Things had begun well, but had rapidly gone downhill…

On the first day of the first term in the very first lesson it had all looked so promising. Fairy Godmother welcomed them.

"Young fairies," she boomed. "Welcome to the School of Nine Wishes. I hope you will all be very happy here. Now, who can tell me why you are here?"

Felicity instantly put up her hand. She knew the answer. She was quite beside herself, she actually knew the answer!

Fairy Godmother was delighted to see such a keen young fairy.

"What's your name, dear?" she asked.

"Felicity," said Felicity proudly. "Felicity Wishes."

"So, Felicity Wishes, tell the class why you are here at the School of Nine Wishes."

"Because," said Felicity, "we got

a letter telling us to come."

A slight giggle rippled through the classroom. Fairy Godmother struggled to keep a straight face and paused before composing herself. "That's true, Felicity," she said. Felicity was just about to beam with delight that she had got the answer right when Fairy Godmother added, "but it wasn't quite the answer I was looking for. Can anyone else help?"

Felicity's friend Polly put her hand up and said, "We're here to learn all the skills we need to become fully qualified fairies,

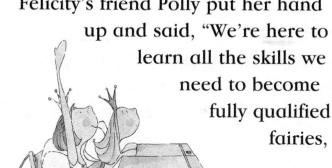

so that we can go out into the world and use our magical powers for the good of others."

"Beautifully put!" said Fairy Godmother, clapping her hands. "That, young fairies, in a nutshell, is why you are all here!"

Felicity didn't hear anything else Fairy Godmother said after that. Her cheeks were burning hot with embarrassment and she hung her head so low her crown nearly fell off.

"How awful!" she said to Daisy, after the class. "I must have set some kind of school record for getting the answer wrong to the first question of the first lesson of the first class on the first day of the first term!"

"You didn't get it *wrong*, Felicity," said Daisy.

"I didn't get it *right*," mumbled Felicity, "or why did Fairy Godmother put the question to the class again?"

"It just wasn't the answer she was looking for, that's all," said Daisy. "It's nothing to worry about."

But Felicity *was* worried. How did you know what answer was required if there wasn't always a right one or a wrong one?

After finally managing to drag herself out of bed, Felicity sat down to eat her breakfast. She thought about her school report again.

"Concentrate more, that's the key," she said to herself, wiping the milk moustache from her mouth. The problem was, it was so easy to get distracted!

* * *

After school assembly, where the fairies sang like angels only much

better, Felicity, Polly, Holly and Daisy
trooped off to the science lab.

Inside, there were row upon row
of shimmering glass test tubes in
holders, carefully labelled bottles
of every colour sparkle you could
imagine, shiny silver spatulas, pots
of coloured crystals with names
such as Frosted Juniper, Preserved
Snowflakes and Star Dust. The
science teacher, Miss Crystal, moved
from desk to desk ticking off the
items on her clipboard. This was
obviously going to be a special
science lesson!

"Fairies!" she announced. "Today,
we are going to have our first attempt
at making magic sparkle dust." The

room buzzed with excitement. This was a taste of what they had come to school for – to learn how to be proper fairies.

"Settle down, settle down!" said Miss Crystal, laughing. "Those of you who manage to get some useable dust can take it into your next class for your practical wish lesson."

Even *more* exciting! Making sparkle dust and then actually being able to use it!

Miss Crystal continued, "Everything you need is on the workbench. We're only going to make quite weak sparkle dust as this is your first attempt. The instructions are clearly written out for you. See how you get on and let me know if there is a part you don't understand."

Felicity looked at the instructions. They made absolutely no sense to her at all.

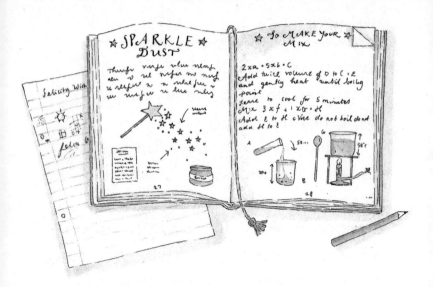

Felicity looked around her.

Everyone else seemed to be counting out spatulas of powder and measuring liquids into test-tubes already. There was much sniffing and stirring and pouring and shaking and watching and waiting. Miss Crystal had told them to ask if they didn't understand something, but how could Felicity confess that she didn't understand ANYTHING?

Polly was waiting for her mixture to boil. Out of the corner of her eye, she noticed Felicity looking like a startled rabbit.

"Are you alright, Felicity?" she asked her puzzled friend.

"I have NO IDEA what to do, Polly," said Felicity, wrinkling her nose. "No idea even where to start!"

"Don't look at the whole equation – it looks really scary at first," said Polly. "Take it step by step. Start with two spatulas of the stuff in bottle A and five spatulas from the jar labelled B. That makes a mixture Miss Crystal is calling C."

Suddenly it all seemed to make sense! It was just like following a recipe.

Felicity had spent so much time worrying, she was now very behind. She'd have to rush to catch up.

First she picked up a bottle of the most beautiful white powder. This was made from pressed and dried frost crystals, and looked good enough to eat. She quickly mixed the powder with some preserved star dust and added a little morning dew. There was no time to measure. She'd just have to guess.

Felicity glanced over her shoulder. Everyone else looked as if they had almost finished.

"Oh goodness," she thought, turning back to her beaker. "Did I add the morning dew already?"

She'd been so busy looking to see what everyone else had been doing, she'd forgotten what she'd done herself.

"Another one for luck," she said hopefully, as she poured some more morning dew into her beaker and gave it another stir. She popped the glass beaker on the pink tripod and began to heat the mixture. Nothing happened.

"A watched beaker never boils," she told herself, as she started to mix up the next set of ingredients. The mixture turned the most beautiful shade of twinkly blue.

She turned back to her glass beaker on the tripod. Still it wouldn't boil. The others had already poured their mixtures on to glass plates and were waiting for them to cool. Miss Crystal was busy talking to the other fairies and didn't seem to notice Felicity scowling at her still lukewarm mixture.

"Is everyone alright?" called Miss Crystal, above the noise of the class.

"Yes, Miss Crystal!" came back the reply.

"No, Miss Crystal!" muttered Felicity, under her breath.

Felicity decided there was nothing for it but to turn up the heat on the Bunsen burner. The flame roared and soon the golden liquid began to bubble furiously. Excellent! If she *really* hurried she would finish by the end of class and still have some sparkle dust to take to the next lesson.

Felicity looked at the notes: Leave to cool for five minutes. She didn't have time to wait for five minutes. She tried blowing on the liquid, but the steam blew back in her face and made her cough. Perhaps if she poured some out into another flask, that would help it cool down.

She carefully poured some of the steaming liquid into a clean flask. It still seemed very hot. Time was running out. The others were scraping up their golden crystals and spooning them into tiny silk bags.

Daisy and Polly came over to see how Felicity was getting on.

"I'm nearly finished," she said brightly. "All I've got to do is add some of these blue crystals to this golden mixture and I'm there!"

"No, Felicity!" said Polly in a slight panic. "You have to add the golden liquid to the blue crystals.

Not the other
way round!"

But Felicity didn't hear her. She had
already begun to add the blue crystals
to the still hot flask of golden liquid.
There was the most tremendous
gurgling sound, like someone
burping over and over again.

"EVERYONE DUCK!"
shrieked Polly, who,
with Daisy, had
crouched under
the bench.

Suddenly the mixture let out the loudest burp of the lot and a cloud of green bubbles emerged like an erupting volcano from the flask. Green bubbles began to fill the classroom. No-one could see anything of Felicity other than the top of her pink crown.

Miss Crystal rushed to open the window and the bubbles floated out of the classroom and up and away across the playing fields.

Felicity stood dripping wet and bright green from the liquid sparkle dust.

After making sure that it was only Felicity's pride that was hurt, Miss Crystal sent everyone to the cloakroom to clean themselves up. She asked Felicity to stay behind. Felicity was now weeping, huge tears plopping gently on to the bench.

"What happened, Felicity?" asked Miss Crystal gently.

Felicity was sobbing and sniffing at the same time. She didn't have a hanky and couldn't even wipe her nose on her dress because it was covered in stuff which had begun to dry to a green powder which made her sneeze. Miss Crystal gave Felicity her white lace hanky. Felicity blew her nose, wiped her eyes and sobbed. "I didn't know what I was doing at

first and I didn't like to ask. Then
I thought I knew what I was doing
and didn't need to ask. Then I did
what I needed to do so quickly that
I didn't know what I was doing. And
now everyone knows what I've done!"

"I see," said Miss Crystal, who
didn't really see at all but guessed
that Felicity had overheated her
mixture, not let it cool and muddled
up the mixtures at the beginning and
the end. The young fairy looked so
sad it was impossible to be cross.

"Perhaps," thought Miss Crystal to
herself, "I should have paid more

attention to everyone in the class. It's a lesson for me too."

"I don't have any sparkle dust to take to the next class," said Felicity sadly. "That's two classes ruined!"

Miss Crystal pulled out a large silver key which was hanging on a long silver chain around her neck. She walked over to a small plain cupboard on the wall and unlocked it. Suddenly the entire room was filled with a glittery glow. Inside the cupboard were rows and rows of glass bottles. There was a huge bottle labelled Sparkle Dust Practice Grade I, a smaller bottle marked Sparkle Dust Grade II, a very small bottle labelled Super Sparkle Dust – Double Strength, and several others that Felicity couldn't read. There seemed to be enough sparkle dust to make wishes for everyone in the world!

Felicity was open-mouthed with wonder.

"This cupboard is our secret," Miss Crystal said, spooning some dust into one of the little silk bags.

"But won't everyone wonder where I got it from, when science class has just ended so badly?" asked Felicity.

"If anyone asks you where you got it, just tell them it came from your science class and leave it at that. Now, off you go."

Felicity had just got to the door when Miss Crystal called out.

"Felicity! Next time, try to concentrate – and if you get in a muddle, don't be afraid to ask."

And, ever since then, Felicity has always asked, even though she sometimes thinks her questions seem silly. After all, she doesn't want to risk ruining another dress!

it's better to feel
silly and ask
when you're not
sure

than look silly
when you don't !

Spotlight Solo

It was the most exciting event of the school year at the School of Nine Wishes: the annual School Concert.

Fairy Godmother had announced the date weeks ago during assembly.

"Young fairies," she boomed to the crowd of eager young faces, their wings quivering with anticipation, "the school concert will be held three weeks from today. Organise yourself into groups. Each group will have five minutes in which to entertain the audience."

Holly was beside herself.

"My chance to show what I can do!" she said to her friends, as they huddled together at first break to discuss what they were going to do. She took a deep breath and announced, "I can smell stardom already!"

"That's the school dinners cooking," said Felicity, wrinkling her nose.

Polly butted in. "Are we going to do

this together as a group, or not?" she asked her friends.

Holly tossed her hair, put her hands on her hips and said with a flourish, "I have to do a solo. I just have to. It's my big chance to be..." she paused, looked up at the sky and said in a ridiculously husky voice, "noticed."

The other three dissolved into giggles. Holly was so over the top. If she was like this three weeks before the performance, what would she be like on the actual day?

Polly would be quite content painting scenery or helping the others learn their lines, so she was very happy to leave the spotlight to Holly. "Don't worry," she said, "you'll get your solo spot. Now, what else are we going to do with our five minutes of fame?"

Daisy said she'd written a poem

entitled, 'The Magic of Flowers', which, if the others agreed, she'd like to read aloud. The others thought this was a good idea, even Holly, who was still planning her own solo act.

"After all," she thought, "it's down to star quality."

The fairies decided that the best plan was for Daisy to read her poem first, then all four of them would perform a dance routine to a song that they would write together. Holly could sing a solo verse in the middle, then they would all join in for the final verse. Polly didn't like the thought of being on stage on her own, and Felicity didn't seem to mind one way or the other, as long as she was with her friends, so it seemed like the perfect solution.

Writing the song proved rather more
difficult.

Dreamy Daisy wanted
something soft and gentle with
a nice tune. Polly thought that
anything that didn't give Daisy a fit
of the giggles would be a start.
Felicity wanted something disco so
she could wear her spangly skirt
and do star jumps, and Holly – well,
Holly thought that if she was going
to sing the solo it was only fair for
her to choose the style she felt most
comfortable with. Which was opera.
The others groaned.

The four friends sat looking at
the white piece of paper in front of

them. They'd been going round in circles for ages and still couldn't decide.

"Let's be sensible," said Polly. "Do any of us play any musical instruments?" Polly saw Felicity's mouth begin to open and quickly added, "Other than the recorder?"

The fairies agreed that their skills were limited. Neither opera nor disco was exactly suited to the recorder, and dancing with a recorder in your mouth would definitely end in tears.

"So," Polly continued, "we've got limited musical ability and we have to write a song. Can I suggest that we choose a tune we all know and write some words to go with it? How about using the melody to 'Twinkle Twinkle Little Star'?"

Felicity thought this was a lovely idea. Daisy was so tired from giggling she would agree to anything. Holly

was already working out how she
could transform the simple tune into
something fit for a fairy diva.

The three weeks since Fairy
Godmother had announced the date
of the concert had flown by and there

were now only twenty-four hours to go. It was time for the first full dress rehearsal!

All day, fairies had been rushing about with paints and paintbrushes, glitter and sequins, pins and needles, instruments, scripts and sheets of music. From inside classrooms came the sound of fairies singing, performing sketches, squeaky scale practice, nervous laughter and frantic cries for lost scripts. If you listened carefully, you could even hear one brave fairy practising her jokes. The whole school buzzed with excitement and anticipation.

The four friends had particular reason to be excited. Having heard them practising during their breaks, Fairy Godmother had asked them to close the show. Polly, Felicity and Daisy's stars nearly pinged off the ends of their wands when they heard. Only Holly remained icy cool.

"I'm not surprised," she said casually, when her friends asked her why she wasn't bouncing up and down with joy. "True talent will always be recognised."

Felicity had stayed up late every

night to make each
of them dresses for
their performance
and was very
pleased with
the result. She'd
found a pattern for an extra super
full skirt with a little matching top.
She'd made the straps out of tiny
gold stars stitched together.

Each of her fairy friends had
chosen their own colour of material.

As Felicity was making the dresses,
she got first choice and chose pink.
Daisy wanted green. Polly chose a
twinkly shade of yellow and Holly
checked the colour of the scenery
around the stage and thought a
deep red would help her stand out.

Felicity cut the pattern out of each
length of material. This was the
trickiest part. One wrong snip could
have them all wearing mini-skirts!

Every night Felicity's sewing machine had whirred. She had pinned and tacked and sewn hand stitches so tiny, she often lost her place. She embroidered tiny gold stars so the outfits looked as if they had been dusted with magic sparkle, and, as a special surprise, she sewed an extra large star right on the front of Holly's dress.

The fairies were thrilled when they saw their outfits.

"You're so good at sewing!" exclaimed Daisy.

"You're the *real* star of the show," said Polly, hugging her friend. "We're going to look magical on stage!"

Even Holly, still trying to remain cool (but whose tummy was doing somersaults inside), couldn't help giving a little skip when she saw the star on her dress.

✳ ✳ ✳

With only half an hour until they were due on stage for rehearsal, Felicity was listening to Daisy recite her poem. Daisy knew it off by heart, but was so nervous she wanted to go over it again and again.

"You know what would have been really lovely?" said Felicity. "With a name like Daisy and a poem about flowers, I should have made you a daisy costume with a skirt of petals."

Daisy agreed. "Oh, Felicity, what a lovely idea, that would have been perfect. What a shame we didn't think of it earlier!"

Felicity looked at her watch. Less than half-an-hour before they were due on stage for rehearsal. Super seamstress Felicity still had time to make Daisy blossom!

Daisy wasn't so sure. Was there

really enough time? But Felicity was already rushing around like a fairy possessed. She found some scissors, a net curtain, glue and some yellow ribbon, and got to work. A hundred beautiful petals fell from the curtain as she snipped, and then, as there wasn't time to sew, she glued them all, one by one, layer upon layer, to the ribbon, so they hung down in gentle, transparent layers. It looked magical!

"Take off your skirt, turn around and close your eyes," Felicity said to Daisy, who was still reciting her poem under her breath.

Daisy undid her skirt and Felicity tied the petal-laden ribbon around Daisy's waist. It looked lovely. "There!" she said. "Open your eyes. A daisy for Daisy! You can wear this for your poem, and then pop your dress on over the top for our song." Daisy was speechless.

Just at that moment, Daisy's name was called. With shaky wings she made her way to the centre of the stage. If she were this wobbly for the rehearsal, what would she be like for the real thing?

The lights were bright and extremely hot. Just as Daisy took an extra deep breath to begin her poem, a fairy from the side signalled for her to stop – there was a problem with one of the lights. She stood patiently and waited for the wave to carry on. Just when she thought her little wings couldn't stand the heat

any longer she was given the
sign to continue.

Daisy began her poem
beautifully. She was
concentrating so hard,
she didn't feel
the petals
on her skirt
falling off
one by
one.

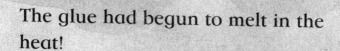

The glue had begun to melt in the
heat!

The petals were so light that when they fell to reveal her little green tights, they didn't make a sound. It was only at the end when Daisy tried to find the corners of her skirt to curtsey, that she realised she had no skirt left to curtsey with!

Daisy wanted to hide forever with embarrassment.

"It was a disaster," she sighed.

"At least you were wearing your tights!" said Felicity, who felt a little responsible. "Everyone loved your outfit. I'll hand sew it for the real performance."

It was time for the four friends to rehearse their song. Polly had written the words to go along with 'Twinkle Twinkle Little Star' and the original idea had been that all four of them would start on stage, with Holly stepping forward to sing her solo in the spotlight before they all joined in for the final verse. Holly wanted to make more of an entrance though, and decided not to appear on stage until the point of her solo.

The rehearsal of the song was uneventful and they all went home humming, "Fairies of the world unite…"

Felicity was still humming as she worked late into the night, sewing each petal on to Daisy's skirt by hand, so that she wouldn't droop tomorrow.

* * *

The day of the concert. The fairies had made a make-shift dressing room in one of the classrooms and had propped up mirrors on the desks. Everyone had sent each other 'Good Luck' cards, although Holly had written 'Break a Leg' on hers, which the others thought strange.

"It's what theatre people do!" said Holly excitedly.

Fairy Godmother was sitting in the front row, together with other grand-looking fairies with wings larger than any of them had ever seen.

"There are so many fairies out there!" whispered Felicity, peeping out from behind the curtain.

"Don't tell me!" said Polly, her wings more of a flutter now than they had ever been.

* * *

The other fairies did their pieces with sparkle, smiles and small mishaps, but always to great applause.

It was almost time for their performance! They'd all been so nervous watching from the wings it was some time before Felicity noticed that Holly was missing. She looked around and asked some of the others, but none of them had seen Holly.

Daisy was about to go on. It would soon be time for them all to perform.

"You go on," Felicity said to Daisy. "I'll go and look for Holly."

"Don't be long, will you?" Polly said nervously.

* * *

Felicity found Holly sitting in front of the mirror in the classroom, a huge towel wrapped around her head.

"Holly! Thank goodness! Didn't you realise it's almost time for us to go on stage?"

Holly remained seated, staring into the mirror.

"I can't go on, I can't go on!" she wailed.

Felicity was shocked. Holly had seemed the calmest of them all – and here she was suffering from stage-fright!

"My career, it's over, OVER!" she continued, throwing her hands in the air.

Felicity crouched at her friend's feet and patted her knee.

"Holly, you'll be fine," she said gently. "You know you were born to perform."

"No!" moaned Holly. "I mean, I really *can't* go on stage. Look!" Holly whipped the towel off her head and there, stuck in her hair at a right angle to her head, was her hairbrush.

Holly cried tears of frustration. "I tried to give my hair an extra big curl at the end and I twirled the brush too tightly," she said miserably. "It's stuck!"

Felicity tried to pull the brush out but Holly screamed "YEOWW!" so loudly she thought the audience was sure to have heard her. When Felicity suggested they cut the brush out of Holly's hair she shouted even louder: "NO!"

Faintly, in the background, Felicity could hear Daisy announce the title of her poem, 'The Magic of Flowers'. There was no time to lose.

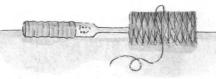

Strand by strand, Felicity carefully teased out Holly's hair from the brush, whilst Holly, now lost in desperate thoughts of a life without fame, covered her eyes.

Daisy was coming to the end of her poem. Polly put her head round the door in a panic.

"The show must go on!" said Felicity to her startled friend. "Just start without me."

Strand after strand she pulled, ordering Holly to keep her head straight and ignoring her yelps of pain. If she worked quickly there might just be time for Holly to make her solo.

The final piece of hair fell free and the fairies rushed to the wings just in time to hear Polly and Daisy finishing their verse.

"It's time for your big moment, your solo, Holly - go for it!" whispered Felicity, pushing her friend out on to the stage. But as she did so, Holly grabbed Felicity's hand and pulled her on to the stage behind her. The two friends stood together, holding hands in the spotlight, and sang. Then all four

of them linked hands for the final
verse. The audience went wild and
there were cries of "More, more!"
so the friends sang the last verse
again, this time with the
audience joining in.

Taking their curtseys, they skipped off the stage and into the wings, where they all hugged each other so hard their crowns popped off.

"I'm so sorry you didn't get a solo," said Felicity to Holly. "I know how important it was to you."

Holly was beaming. "Without you, Felicity, I would have missed my solo altogether! A duet with a best friend is just as good. In fact," she paused, "much better."

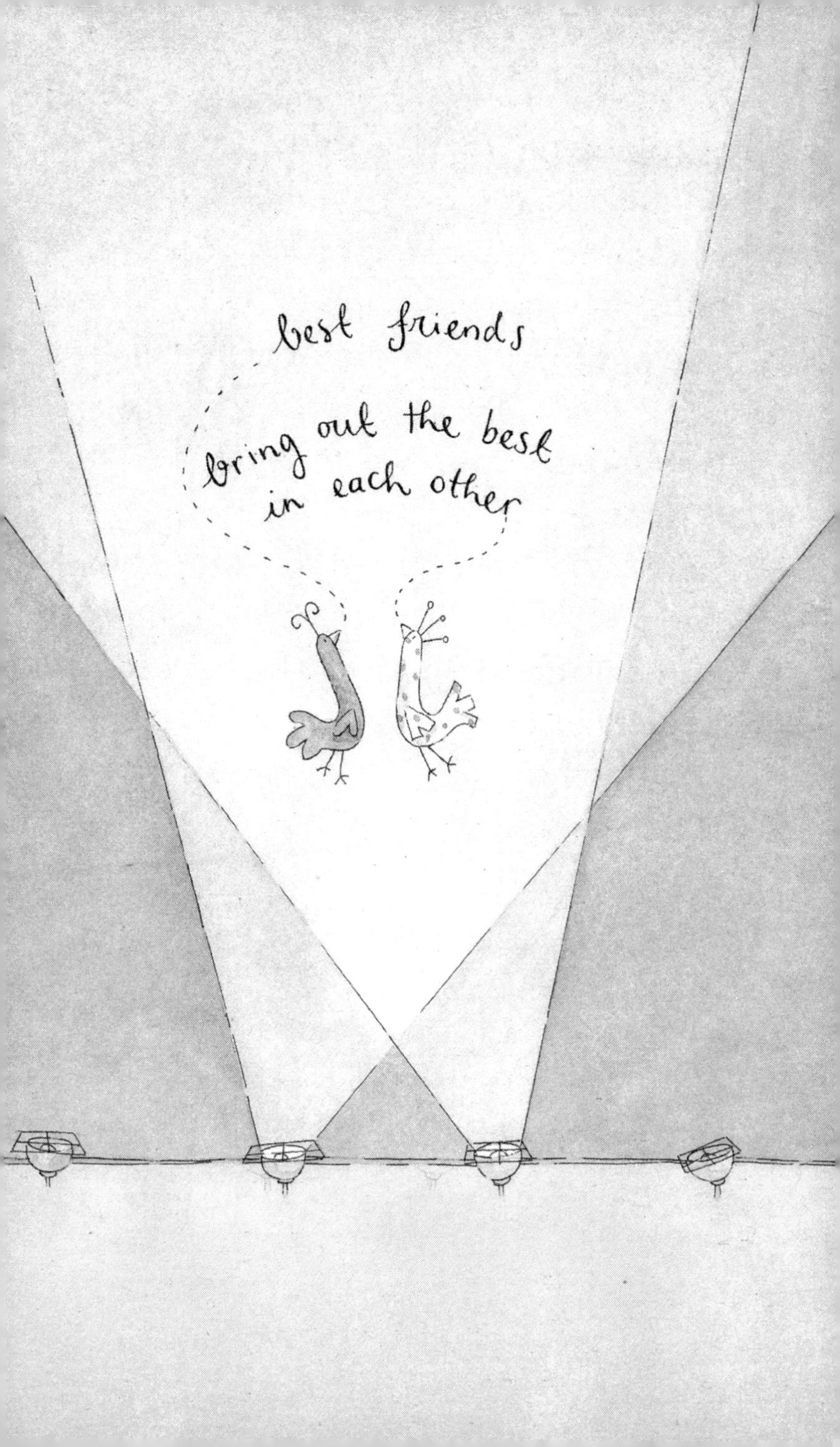
best friends
bring out the best
in each other

Dancing Dreams

It was Friday evening, and a trip to
the ballet had been arranged for the
students of Madame Plié's Dancing

School to see a performance of *Swan Lake*. Everyone was very excited – no one more so than Felicity Wishes. Everything about going to the ballet made her tingle with excitement: the sound of the orchestra tuning up, the muffled chatter of the crowd waiting for the performance to begin, the seats with their plump red velvet cushions, the gold cherubs with their beautiful, feathery wings painted on the ceiling, but most of all, the thought of what lay behind the huge velvet curtain.

Holly had dashed into the theatre the moment Madame Plié had handed over the tickets, and was now lying across four seats keeping them all for her friends. Felicity, Daisy and Polly arrived and sank into their seats. They all began to read the programmes that Madame Plié passed down the row.

Inside was a picture of the
famous Prima Fairy Ballerina,
Natasha Milletova, who delighted
audiences all over the world with
her exquisite dancing. It was said
that she was the most talented
ballerina in living memory, and

that to see her perform was a once in a lifetime opportunity. Tickets for all the performances had been sold out for months, and fairies were still queuing outside the theatre in the hope that a seat would become available at the last moment.

The fairies opened their packets of sweets and the orchestra began to tune their instruments. A bell sounded. The performance was about to begin! A few latecomers dashed in, and Felicity and the others had to tuck their legs in under their skirts and hold their breath so they could get past. Daisy cringed as she saw the person next to her sit on the chocolate truffle she had accidentally dropped. Holly nudged her and giggled. Then the lights dimmed, the orchestra started and the curtain went up with a tremendous swish...

From the first pirouette, Felicity thought *Swan Lake* was the most wonderful ballet she had ever seen and Natasha Milletova the most beautiful ballerina imaginable.

Her wing control was astounding. She could fly across the stage effortlessly, her wings barely appearing to move. She swooped and dived and hovered and spun with breathtaking grace and ease, her tiny silver ballet shoes twinkling magically under the lights. No wonder it was rumoured that she dipped her feet in a tray of magic dust before a performance.

Felicity wanted the evening to go on forever!

When the curtain finally came down at the end of the performance, the audience rose to their feet and clapped and cheered. Even Madame Plié forgot to look stern and smiled broadly and clapped enthusiastically. The curtain rose again and Natasha swept back

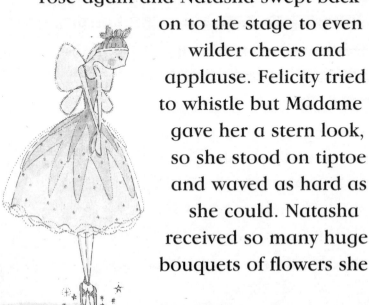

on to the stage to even wilder cheers and applause. Felicity tried to whistle but Madame gave her a stern look, so she stood on tiptoe and waved as hard as she could. Natasha received so many huge bouquets of flowers she could hardly carry them all, and people were throwing so many flowers from the audience it looked as if she was standing on a carpet of blooms. Felicity was sure that Natasha had given her a special smile.

After many encores the curtain finally came down and the lights went up.

The magic had ended.

The young fairies trooped out into the street, pointing their toes and fluttering their wings to the music still in their heads. It had been the best trip to the ballet Felicity could ever remember.

* * *

On Saturday morning, the fairies gathered at the dancing school. Most of them were still chattering about *Swan Lake*, but Felicity was still dreaming about it. All she could think about were the bright lights, the applause and the sight of Natasha Milletova in her tutu and silver shoes giving her a special smile. If only she could dance as well as Natasha.

"Young fairies!" barked Madame Plié, clapping her hands. "Everyone to the middle of the room and assume the first position. We will start with some gentle exercises moving through the positions."

Holly, Polly, Daisy and the other fairies carefully followed Madame Plié's instructions, but Felicity was

too busy dreaming about *Swan Lake*. Although she started in first position she was still in it when the others had moved on to fourth!

"Felicity," whispered Daisy, as her arms swung past Felicity's into fifth position. "Are you stuck? You haven't moved!"

Madame Plié, who hadn't noticed Felicity, heard Daisy and snapped her fingers.

"I won't have talking in my class," she said to Daisy, who blushed the colour of a red rose.

Then Madame saw Felicity, who was standing with her feet in first position and her arms in third.

"Is there a reason why you aren't keeping up, Felicity?" asked Madame.

Felicity didn't hear her. In her head she was Natasha Milletova in the final scenes of *Swan Lake*.

Daisy nudged Felicity, who suddenly realised the entire class was staring at her.

"Sorry, Madame Plié," said Felicity. "I'll try to keep up."

"Please concentrate," said Madame, clearly irritated. "Concentration is extremely important in ballet. Perfect performances start with simple steps!"

Felicity didn't understand what Madame meant, but whatever Madame had said, Felicity's performance in class didn't get any better.

When they moved to the barre to practise their pliés, the long line of fairies rose and fell to the gentle tinkle of the music, all except Felicity, who managed to fall when everyone else had risen. In one exercise, Felicity still had her leg in front of her when the others moved theirs behind.

"I didn't mean to kick Daisy in the bottom!" she explained sheepishly, as the fairies untangled their legs from the mess her mistake had made.

Finally, the class came to an end. Tutu's, tights and shoes were packed away and, giggling and chattering, the class began to empty. Felicity was still in her ballet clothes when Polly called over, "Are you coming to Sparkles for a hot chocolate with us, Felicity?"

"Er…yes," said Felicity vaguely.

There was always a scramble for chairs and tables at the café when class was over and the fairies didn't want to wait.

"We'll go on and get a table," said Polly, heading out of the door.

"Don't be long!" called Daisy, over her shoulder.

When her friends had gone, Felicity began to look at the pictures of famous Prima Fairy Ballerinas which were hanging on the wall. Each one looked poised and beautiful.

There was even a picture of a young Madame Plié, so-called because her pliés were so low her knees almost touched the floor. Felicity couldn't imagine Madame Plié being a young fairy, let alone being able to bend her knees very far.

Seeing photographs of the ballerinas brought back memories of the night before. The music came flooding back into her head.

She could smell the flowers, hear the

orchestra and see Natasha Milletova
come shimmering on to the stage.

Felicity began to dance, pretending
that she was Natasha, hearing the
audience gasp with delight as she
performed. Faster and faster she
danced, throwing herself around
the room.

As she was
heading
towards the
grand finale
she attempted
a mid-air
pirouette,
began spinning
so fast she
became dizzy, lost
her bearings
and ricocheted
off the wall,
before landing
on the chandelier
hanging from the ceiling.
"Golly," thought
Felicity. "I think I got
a bit over-excited there."
But when she tried
to untangle herself from
the chandelier she found
she was stuck. Her wings

were wedged tight and the
ribbons from her shoes
had come undone
and were wound
round the crystal droplets.

"Hello?" Felicity called out.
"Is there anyone there?"
But the room below was
empty. All her friends had
left to go to Sparkles and
Madame Plié was nowhere
to be seen. What on earth was
Felicity going to do? She could
be here all night!

Every time she moved, the chandelier
tinkled prettily and made beautiful
rainbow patterns on the wall but, try
as she might, she couldn't wriggle
herself free.

"Help!" Felicity called at last."Help!"
There was no answer.
The room was completely silent.

* * *

After what seemed like hours (but was probably only a few minutes), the door opened and in walked a tiny figure wearing woolly socks and a woolly jumper over a pair of grey tights.

Felicity was about to shout "HELP!" when she realised that the fairy below her was none other than Natasha Milletova.

Felicity couldn't believe it! Prima Fairy Ballerina Milletova below her in Madame Plié's Dancing School! She couldn't possibly ask the world famous ballerina to remove her from a chandelier. It would be just TOO embarrassing.

To Felicity's amazement, Natasha walked to the centre of the room and began to do the same exercises that Madame Plié had been doing with the class earlier that day. Where were the amazing arabesques and perfect

pirouettes that Felicity and her friends
had seen on stage?

First position, second position, third
position, fourth and fifth. Several
times she went through this routine,
watching herself in the mirrors around
the room.

Felicity could feel her nose
beginning to twitch. The chandelier
was very dusty.

"Oh no!" thought Felicity in a panic,
"I'm going to sneeze!"

"ATISHOO!" Felicity sneezed so hard
the chandelier tinkled like a
thousand raindrops falling.

Natasha looked up sharply
at the young fairy hanging
helplessly from the light.

"I'm so sorry," Felicity
shouted down. "I'm stuck!"

Natasha flew up to Felicity
and quickly untangled her wings
and unwound the ribbons from

her shoes. Felicity felt a bit dizzy from hanging upside down, so Natasha held her hand as they flew back down.

"Are you alright?" enquired the Prima Ballerina, finding Felicity a chair to sit on. "How on earth did you start a ballet class and end up tangled in a chandelier?"

Felicity blushed. How could she tell Natasha that after seeing *Swan Lake* she had been daydreaming in her ballet class about being her, and had got carried away? It was so embarrassing. This was Natasha Milletova!

But Felicity was feeling too dizzy to think of a tale tall enough to save her blushes, so she bit her lip and told the truth.

"I couldn't believe it when you came in," said Felicity shyly. "I *thought* it was you, but then when I saw you do the same exercises we do in class I thought it couldn't possibly be."

Natasha smiled at Felicity, who was glowing with rosy cheeks.

"All dancers, whatever level, must start with exercises," said Natasha. "It warms up our muscles so we don't get injured."

"But what about the flying arabesques?" asked Felicity. "What about the fun stuff?"

Natasha began to laugh. "The fun stuff is actually very hard work. You know all the movements you see on stage?"

Felicity nodded enthusiastically.

"Each one of those has its beginnings in the exercises you do as a young fairy. The more experienced you get, the more you put the exercises together to make something magical."

So *that* was what Madame Plié had been meaning when she'd said, "Perfect performances start with simple steps."

"But what are you doing here?" asked Felicity. Even with her woolly tights and jumper Natasha still seemed impossibly glamorous.

"I'm dancing in *The Nutcracker* this evening," said Natasha. "I wanted to get away from the theatre and go through some steps in peace and quiet. Madame said I could use the room after your class had finished. I didn't expect to have an audience!"

"I'm sorry," said Felicity. "I'll leave you alone. Thank you so much for helping me."

"I don't know your name," said Natasha, as Felicity headed for the door.

"Felicity," said Felicity quietly. "Felicity Wishes."

Natasha reached into her bag and, after some searching, pulled out a pair of tiny, silver ballet shoes, which

she handed to Felicity. Felicity's
mouth fell open as she recognised
them.

"Are they really the ones you wore
"Yes," she asked

"Yes," she asked Natasha, ready
heading back to the fire. "Now off
you go, so I can prac. I'm sure
I'll see you again so"

Felicity didn't hear, she was so
busy saying thank y. Then she
flew as fast as she uld to Sparkles.
What a wonderful t! What a once
in a lifetime meetin. The others
were never going to
believe it!

When Felicity finally got to the café she showed her friends the tiny silver shoes.

"There's something tucked inside," said Holly, peering at them closely. Felicity read the four tickets for that evening's performance of The Nutcracker. It was only that she remembered Natasha's parting words. She really would be seeing her again soon!

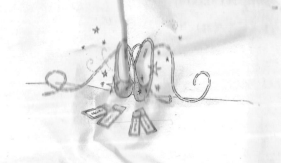

the most magical
surprises

always turn up in
the most unexpected
places !

Collect all four Felicity Wishes story collections:

＊ ＊ ＊

Fashion Fiasco

Dancing Dreams

Spooky Sleepover

Wand Wishes

＊